You're the main character. You make the choices.
# Can You Survive?

Sir Arthur Conan Doyle's
Adventures of
# Sherlock Holmes

adapted by
Ryan Jacobson and Deb Mercier

Minneapolis, Minnesota

# Dedication

For Dana, friend and mystery buff.

—Ryan

For Jay, my partner down all life's paths.

—Deb

# Acknowledgements

A special thanks to Corrine and the {Teen} Book Scene.

Edited by Blake Hoena
Cover art by David Hemenway

10 9 8 7 6 5 4 3 2 1

Copyright 2011 by Ryan Jacobson and Deb Mercier
Published by Lake 7 Creative, LLC
Minneapolis, MN 55412
www.lake7creative.com

ISBN: 978-0-9774122-4-2

# Dear Reader,

Do you like to read? Do you love video games? If so, I think you're really going to enjoy this book. I've loved choose your path books since I was in fifth grade, and I'm excited to share one with you now.

I have to admit: I was never into mysteries as a child. But I've grown to love them. And, of course, Sherlock Holmes is the world's greatest detective. He's brilliant, he's cool, and he's (almost) always right. Of late, I've been devouring his stories both in book form and on my TV screen.

Sir Arthur Conan Doyle's *The Adventures of Sherlock Holmes* is a collection of short stories. Deb and I have selected a few favorites and adapted them into this choose your path book, giving you the opportunity to test your detective skills against those of Sherlock Holmes, himself.

We have taken great care to keep much of Doyle's own writing intact, but consider this book a short introduction to *The Adventures of Sherlock Holmes*. When you reach a time, now or in the future, where it is appropriate for you to do so, I encourage you to read *The Adventures of Sherlock Holmes* in its entirety. For now, I hope this version will do.

—Ryan Jacobson

# How to Use This Book

As you read *Sir Arthur Conan Doyle's Adventures of Sherlock Holmes*, you will sometimes be asked to jump to a distant page. Please follow these instructions. Sometimes you will be asked to choose between two or more options. Decide which you feel is best, and go to the corresponding page. (But be careful; some of the options will lead to disaster.) Finally, if a page offers no instructions or choices, simply turn to the next page.

Enjoy the story, and good luck!

# Table of Contents

# Prologue

You sit in your study room, on the top floor of your uncle's three-story house. You hate coming here. There are no games, no televisions, no computers—and the whole place smells like bad breath. For the next three hours, it's just you and your homework. Right now, it's math. Word problems are the worst.

You've been reading and re-reading the same exact question for at least 20 minutes. "Ugh, I can't do this!" you shout, throwing your pencil against the wall.

You push away from your desk and lean down to pick up your pencil. That's when you hear a jangle of hums and crashes. It seems to be coming from the room next door. You follow the noise to the cramped bathroom, just big enough for a toilet, a sink, and a place to stand in between. You squeeze inside and discover that the sound is above you. You look up and notice the attic entrance: a square opening in the ceiling, covered by a wooden panel.

You should probably leave this mystery alone and get back to studying. But it is a welcome distraction. Anything is better than math homework.

You climb onto the sink and reach upward. The panel pops out of place as you push it. A cloud of dust wafts into your face, causing you to cough and sneeze.

You slide the panel aside, and you reach through the opening. You carefully pull yourself up—your hands, your elbows, your waist, your knees. Safely inside, you climb onto your feet. The air is thick with dust. The floor is crowded with old boxes, trunks, and bookshelves.

From the corner to your right, the peculiar sound rings loudly. You creep toward it, trying to keep the rickety old floor from creaking. As you draw closer, the noise becomes clearer.

You hear screams, shouts and the echoes of gunfire, sounds of an adventure. The bizarre commotion leads you to a shelf lined with crumbly, battered books: *The Call of the Wild, Treasure Island, 20,000 Leagues Under the Sea* and more. But the sounds seem to be coming from one book in particular: Sir Arthur Conan Doyle's *The Adventures of Sherlock Holmes*.

You're afraid to guess what will happen if you pick up the book, yet you can't help feeling curious. Could this be the thrill of a lifetime? Will it be dangerous? Is there a chance you'll get hurt, or worse? You feel strangely certain that the answer is "yes" to all of the above.

The sound slowly begins to fade. Your instincts tell you it's now or never. You must decide, and you must decide fast. Will you pick up the book, or will you leave it be? What will you choose to do?

To pick up the book, turn to page 32.

To return to studying, turn to page 69.

You spring out and grab the intruder by the collar.

"Great Scott! Jump, Archie, jump," he shouts.

The other man dives down the hole. You hear the sound of tearing cloth as Jones clutches at his jacket.

You release John Clay and level the barrel of your revolver at him. "It's no use, John Clay," you tell him. "You have no chance at all."

Mr. Merryweather hides behind a crate. Watson and Jones peer into the hole in the floor.

Clay smiles coldly. In a flash of motion, he knocks the pistol from your hand. It clinks upon the stone floor. The criminal scoops it up and levels it at you instead.

"Wrong. I believe it is you who has no chance," John Clay snarls.

You hear a thunder-like clap, and you feel a sharp, piercing pain. You crumple to the ground, and then you know no more.

**Turn to page 68.**

"It tells me that you are a member of the order known as the Freemasons," you say.

"Very good, sir!" responds your client.

"And now, Mr. Wilson, tell us all about yourself, your household, and this advertisement. You will make a note, Watson, of the paper and the date."

"It is *The Morning Chronicle* of April 27, 1890. Just two months ago."

"Very good. Now, Mr. Wilson?"

"It is just as I have been telling you, Mr. Holmes," says Mr. Wilson, mopping his forehead. "I have a small pawnbroker's shop at Coburg Square. It's not very large. I used to be able to keep two assistants, but now I only keep one. I can only afford that because he is willing to come for half wages to learn the business."

"What is his name?" you ask.

"Vincent Spaulding. I could not wish for a smarter assistant, Mr. Holmes."

"You seem most fortunate in having an employee who comes for half wages. It is not common."

"Oh, he has his faults," says Mr. Wilson. "He wastes his time on photography. Snapping away with a camera when he ought to be working. Then he dives down into the cellar to develop his pictures. That is his main fault, but on the whole he's a good worker."

"He is still with you, I presume?"

"Yes, sir. He and a girl who does a bit of cooking and keeps the place clean—that's all I have in the house, for I never had my own family. We live very quietly, sir, the three of us. We keep a roof over our heads and pay our debts, if we do nothing more." Mr. Wilson pauses for a moment before adding, "I see that you've noticed the pink fish tattoo on my wrist. Does it reveal anything?"

You smile at him and say, "One final test, is it? Very well, Mr. Wilson."

If you think the tattoo means Mr. Wilson enjoys eating salmon, turn to page 17.

If you think the tattoo means Mr. Wilson has visited China, turn to page 22.

# The Cunning of John Clay

It is just before ten o'clock when Watson walks into your office. He is perfectly on time.

"Our party is complete," you proclaim. "Watson, you already know Mr. Jones, of Scotland Yard. Allow me to introduce Mr. Merryweather, our companion in tonight's adventure."

"I hope this will not be a wild goose chase," grumbles Mr. Merryweather.

"You may place your confidence in Mr. Holmes," replies the Scotland Yard officer. "He has the makings of a detective in him."

"Oh, if you say so, Mr. Jones, it is all right then," says Mr. Merryweather.

"I think you will find the night worth your while," you assure the men. "For you, Mr. Merryweather, the stake will be three million dollars. For you, Jones, it will be the man you've been tracking for years."

"John Clay, the murderer, thief, and forger," Mr. Jones explains. "I would rather have my handcuffs on him than on any criminal in London. He's a remarkable man, this young John Clay. His brain is as cunning as his fingers. We find clues of him at every turn, but we never know where to find the man himself."

"I hope that I may introduce you tonight," you say. "It is past ten and quite time that we start. If you two will take the first carriage, Watson and I will follow in the second."

**Go to the next page.**

You remain mostly silent during the long drive. The carriage rattles through an endless maze of streets until it turns onto Farrington Street.

"We are close now," you remark. "Merryweather is a bank director and personally interested in the matter. I thought it as well to have Jones with us. He is as brave as a bulldog. Here we are, and they are waiting for us."

You reach the same road that you visited in the morning. Following Mr. Merryweather, you pass down a passage and through a side door, into a small corridor. It ends at a massive iron gate. Mr. Merryweather opens the gate and leads you down a flight of stone steps, to another iron gate.

Mr. Merryweather stops to light a lantern. Then he conducts you down a dark, earth-smelling passage. He opens a third door, revealing a huge vault, which is filled with crates.

"You are not vulnerable from above," you remark, holding up the lantern and gazing upward.

"Nor from below," says Mr. Merryweather. He strikes his stick upon the floor. "Why, dear me, it sounds quite hollow!" he exclaims, looking up in surprise.

"I must really ask you to be a little more quiet!" you snap. "Might I beg that you sit down upon one of those boxes and not to interfere?"

Mr. Merryweather perches himself upon a crate with a hurt expression on his face. You fall onto your knees. With the lantern and a magnifying lens, you examine the cracks between the stones. A few seconds is enough. You spring to your feet again.

"We have at least an hour before us," you remark. "They can hardly take any steps until the pawnbroker is safely in bed. Then they will not lose a minute. The sooner they do their work, the longer they will have for their escape. We are in the cellar of the Coburg Bank. Mr. Merryweather is the director, and he will explain that there are reasons why the criminals of London should take an interest in this cellar."

"Our French gold," whispers the director. "We have had warnings that an attempt might be made upon it."

"Your French gold?" Watson asks.

"We borrowed three million dollars from the Bank of France. It has become known that we have never unpacked the money. It is still lying in our cellar."

"And now it is time that we arrange our little plans," you say. "I expect that, within an hour, matters will come to a head. In the meantime, Mr. Merryweather, we must cover the lanterns."

"And sit in the dark?"

"I am afraid so. I see that the enemy's preparations have gone so far that we cannot risk the presence of a light. Now, we must choose our positions."

You glance around the cellar, looking for a spot. Is it wiser to hide several feet away from the place where John Clay will enter? Or should you crouch directly behind Clay's entrance? If you are farther from him, you will be well hidden. But if you are closer, you will reach the villain more quickly. It is a difficult decision. What will you choose to do?

To hide closer to Clay's entrance, turn to page 64.

To hide farther from the entrance, turn to page 40.

You lean back in your chair, feeling confident in your powers of observation. "Of course, your tattoo can mean only one thing, Mr. Wilson. You are extremely fond of eating salmon, so much so that you had its likeness tattooed on your wrist."

Mr. Wilson's face turns as red as his hair. He stands and points at you with a shaking finger. The pink fish on his wrist jiggles. "Ridiculous, I hate salmon. You, sir, are a fraud!"

He stomps toward the door. He pushes past Watson and then turns back to you. "Everyone will hear of your fraud, Sherlock Holmes. Everyone!"

The door slams behind him. You and Dr. Watson are left in a stunned and awkward silence.

Finally Watson clears his throat. "Well, Holmes, I expect we haven't heard the last of Mr. Jabez Wilson."

**Turn to page 67.**

# Consulting Detective

It is a beautiful summer day in London, England. The year is 1890. You stand inside your home office at 221B Baker Street. Your front door bears the words, "Sherlock Holmes, Consulting Detective."

Dr. John H. Watson stands with you. He has been your trusted assistant for years. Before that, he served as a doctor in the British military. He is shorter and rounder than you, and his skills in the art of deduction are lacking. But he is a good man, and he has saved your life on many occasions.

"I know, my dear Watson, that you share my love of all that is bizarre," you announce.

"Of course, Holmes," he replies. "This very morning,

three such cases have presented themselves. You must select the one that you first wish to address."

"I will do just that."

"Before I continue," Dr. Watson adds, "I must pass along a warning from your friend Mr. Jones of Scotland Yard. He has reason to believe that your rival, Professor Moriarty, has set a trap. I fear one of these cases may be a trick which could cost you your life. Yet neither Mr. Jones nor I can guess which it might be."

"Well, then," you say with a confident grin, "please spare no detail. I must learn all there is about each."

**Go to the next page.**

"The first comes from a Mr. Jabez Wilson," your friend announces. "He claims to be a member of the Red-headed League."

"And what is the Red-headed League?" you ask.

"I do not know," Watson answers. "Mr. Wilson said only that he wishes you to help him investigate it."

"Quite interesting," you say. "The matter seems far too whimsical for the rigid, logical mind of Moriarty."

"Indeed," Watson agrees. "The second case involves a young woman named Helen Stoner. She tells that her sister died quite mysteriously some two years ago. She now fears that her own life is in peril."

"Ah, this sounds like a trap," you declare. "Yet, a damsel in distress is a bit cliché. It is so obviously a trap that I doubt it truly is."

Watson scratches his head. "If you say so, Holmes."

"Tell me about the third case."

"A young military man, Tom Rairy, claims to be someone of great importance. He was rather secretive, but he said that his work has been met with foul play. Someone has sabotaged him. He wishes for you to help him find the culprit."

"Ha! Another interesting petition. I do believe that this one, like the last, is too obvious a scheme for the cunning mind of Professor Moriarty. Are you certain one of these is a false claim?"

"Not at all, Holmes," Watson admits. "They may each be true. And yet, if one of the choices could put you in jeopardy, it may be wise to decline them all. So tell me, Holmes, what will you choose to do?"

To take Mr. Wilson's case, turn to page 46.

To take Miss Stoner's case, turn to page 72.

To take Mr. Rairy's case, turn to page 88.

To turn them all down, turn to page 60.

"It reveals that you have been to China. The fish could only have been done there," you reply. "I have made a study of tattoo marks. That trick of staining the fishes' scales with a delicate pink is unique to China. I also see a Chinese coin hanging from your watch chain."

Mr. Wilson laughs heavily. "You are truly as clever as they say, Mr. Holmes."

"In addition, I see that you have done a great amount of writing, but I can deduce nothing else," you add.

"Writing?" he exclaims. "How could you possibly know that?"

"Your right sleeve is shiny for five inches, and the left one has a smooth patch near the elbow where you rest it on the desk," you note. "Shall we return to business?"

Mr. Wilson nods and begins his tale:

*"Spaulding came into the shop eight weeks ago. He told me, 'There's an opening on the League of the Red-headed Men. It's worth quite a little fortune.'*

*"I asked him what the League was. You see, I am a very stay-at-home man.*

*"'Have you never heard of the League of the Red-headed Men?' Spaulding asked. 'You are eligible for the opening.'*

"He went on to say that it's worth several thousand dollars a year, and the work is very simple. It need not interfere much with one's other work. Mr. Holmes, you can imagine that made me listen, for business has not been over-good for some years. Some extra money would have been very handy.

"He showed me the ad and said, 'The League was started by an American millionaire. He was red-headed, and he had a great sympathy for all red-headed men. When he died, he left his fortune in the hands of trustees. They were instructed to apply his money toward men whose hair is of that color.'

"'But,' I said, 'there would be millions of red-headed men who would apply.'

"'Not so many as you might think,' he answered. 'I have heard it is no use applying if your hair is light red, or dark red, or anything but bright, blazing, fiery red. If you cared to apply, Mr. Wilson, you would just walk in.'

"I was convinced. We shut the business up and started off for the address that was given in the advertisement.

"I never hope to see such a sight as that again. From north, south, east, and west, every man who had any red in his hair had answered the advertisement. I would have given it up, but Spaulding would not hear of it. He pushed and pulled until he got me through the crowd and right up to the steps which led to the office. We wedged in as well as we could and soon found ourselves in the office.

"There was nothing inside but a couple of wooden chairs, a table, and a small man with hair even redder than mine. He immediately liked me. He closed the door as we entered so that he might have a private word with us.

"'You have every requirement,' he said. 'I cannot recall when I have seen anything so fine as your hair.' Suddenly he plunged forward, shook my hand, and congratulated me warmly on my success. Then he stepped over to the window and shouted that the job was filled. A groan came up from below, and the folks trooped away in different directions.

"'My name,' he said, 'is Mr. Duncan Ross. When shall you be able to begin your new duties?'

"'Well, it is a little awkward, for I have a business already,' I answered. But Vincent Spaulding told me not to worry. He would be able to look after the business for me.

"'What would be the hours?' I asked.

"'Ten to two.'

"Now, Mr. Holmes, a pawnbroker's business is mostly done in the evening. So it would suit me very well to earn a little in the mornings. Besides, I knew my assistant would see to anything that turned up. I agreed to the job.

"'You have to be in the office, or at least in the building, the whole time,' Mr. Ross warned. 'If you leave, you forfeit your position forever.'

"'It's only four hours a day. I will not think of leaving,' I said. 'And the work?'

"'To write out the Encyclopedia Britannica, word for word. Will you be ready tomorrow?'

"'Certainly,' I answered.

**Go to the next page.**

"In the morning, I found everything there. The table was ready for me, and Mr. Duncan Ross was there to see that I got to work. He started me off upon the letter A, and then he left me. But he would drop in from time to time to see that all was right with me.

"This went on day after day, Mr. Holmes. And then on Saturday the manager came in and paid me for my week's work. It was the same next week, and the same the week after. Eight weeks passed away like this. And then suddenly the whole business came to an end."

**Go to the next page.**

# What's Your Next Move?

"To an end?" you ask.

"Yes, sir. This morning, I went to my work, but the door was locked. A card was tacked onto the middle of the panel. Here it is, and you can read for yourself."

Mr. Wilson holds up a piece of white cardboard the size of a sheet of paper. It reads: THE RED-HEADED LEAGUE IS DISSOLVED. June 27, 1890.

You study this announcement until the comical side tops every other consideration. You burst into a roar of laughter, and Watson does the same.

"I cannot see that there is anything funny," cries your client. "If you can do nothing better than laugh at me, I can go elsewhere."

Mr. Wilson stands to leave, and part of you wishes to let him go. At that moment, your friend Watson leans over and whispers into your ear. "His story is ridiculous. I sense a trap. Your life may be in peril, Holmes."

You cannot help but agree. Mr. Wilson's tale is a bit far-fetched. Could this be a trap set by Moriarty? Should you have this man arrested at once? If you do, you may be rescuing yourself from danger, or you might be missing one of the greatest mysteries of your career. What will you choose to do?

To continue with the case, turn to page 57.

To have Mr. Wilson arrested, turn to page 43.

You spring out of your chair with the gesture of a man who has made up his mind. "Put on your hat and come with me," you tell Watson.

You travel together to Coburg Square, the scene of Mr. Wilson's story. Four rows of brick houses form a square around a small, fenced-in enclosure. At a corner house, a brown board with "JABEZ WILSON" painted in white letters announces the place where your red-headed client works.

You stop in front of the shop and look it over. Then you walk slowly up the street and down again to the corner, still studying the houses. Finally you return to the pawnbroker's. You thump upon the pavement with a stick, two or three times. Then you go up to the door and knock. It is opened by Vincent Spaulding. He asks you to step in.

"I only wish to ask how to get from here to the Strand," you tell Spaulding.

"Third right, fourth left," the assistant answers. Without another word, he closes the door.

"Smart fellow," you observe. "He is, in my judgment, the fourth smartest man in London."

"Evidently," says Watson. "Mr. Wilson's assistant counts for a good deal in this mystery. I am sure that you knocked so you might see him."

"Not him."

"What then?"

"The knees of his pants," you say.

"And what did you see?" asks Watson.

"What I expected to see."

"Why did you beat the pavement?"

"My dear Watson, this is a time for observation, not for talk. We know something of Coburg Square. Let us now explore the parts which lie behind it."

You hurry around the corner to one of the city's main avenues. The roadway is clogged with traffic, while the sidewalks are black with the hurrying swarm of people.

"Let me see," you say, standing at the corner. "I should like to remember the exact order of the houses here. There is Mortimer's, the little newspaper shop, the Coburg Bank, the Vegetarian Restaurant, and McFarlane's carriage depot. And now, Watson, we've done our work. You want to go home, no doubt," you remark.

"Yes, I do," he tells you.

"I have some work which will take several hours. This business at Coburg Square is serious."

"Why serious?"

"A considerable crime is in progress. I have every reason to believe that we are in time to stop it. But today being Saturday complicates matters. I shall want your help tonight at ten o'clock."

"I shall be at your office at ten."

You wave your hand, turn on your heel, and then disappear into the crowd.

**Turn to page 50.**

For you, it's a simple decision. Before the sound dies away, you reach forward and snatch the book off the shelf. It feels old and rough, kind of like a dried out piece of cake.

The sounds grow louder again. The book almost leaps from your hands. You stare at it, gathering your courage. You take a deep breath, hold the book tightly and yank it open.

The room begins to spin. A wind starts to blow. The attic grows blacker and colder. You feel your body being pulled downward. An invisible force pushes you closer to the pages before you. A sharp pain stabs at your forehead.

And then, suddenly, everything is still.

**Turn to page 18.**

You shake your head with a grin. "An obvious fact, you have at some time done manual labor. You have worked with your right hand, and the muscles are more developed."

"Quite right!" Mr. Wilson exclaims. "It's as true as gospel, for I began as a ship's carpenter."

You quickly return to business. "Can you not find the advertisement, Mr. Wilson?"

"Yes, I have it now," he answers. He plants his thick red finger halfway down the newspaper column. "Here it is. This is what began it all."

**Go to the next page.**

# The Red-headed League

*TO THE RED-HEADED LEAGUE: By the request of the late Ezekiah Hopkins of Lebanon, Pennsylvania, USA. There is another job opening; it entitles a member of the League to a salary of $400 a week for very minor services. All red-headed men above the age of 21 years are eligible. Apply in person on Monday, at eleven o'clock, to Duncan Ross, at the offices of the League, 7 Pope's Court, Fleet Street.*

"What on earth does this mean?" exclaims Watson.

You chuckle and wriggle in your chair. "It is a little off the beaten track, isn't it?"

"Indeed, it is Mr. Holmes," says Mr. Wilson. "Before we continue, I wish to request another test."

"Go on, then," you say.

"Have you noticed the pin I wear upon my chest? It is an arc and compass. Does it mean anything to you?"

If it means to you that Mr. Wilson is a member of a private club, turn to page 10.

If it means to you that Mr. Wilson is an airplane pilot, turn to page 49.

You lean forward in your chair. "Watson, the logical course of action is to begin our investigation with Mr. Duncan Ross. He is the key to this peculiar mystery."

"Very good, Holmes," says Watson. "Do you require my assistance?"

"Not yet, my dear Watson, but stay near. Events will progress rather quickly, once I find Mr. Ross."

You walk your friend out the door and then part ways. You study your copy of the advertisement for the Red-headed League. The listed address is not far.

After a short trip, you find yourself in front of a shabby, brick building two stories tall. You open the door and walk into the cool gloom. Just down a narrow hallway you find a door marked "office" and give it a sharp rap.

A short, stout man with a ring of gray hair opens the door and peers up at you. "Yes?" he says.

"Are you the landlord of this building?"

He opens the door wider. "Are you looking to rent?"

"I am investigating a case for a client. I would like to see the office you recently rented out on the second floor, if possible."

The man's eyebrows draw together. "You mean that Red-headed club?"

"Red-headed League, yes," you reply.

"Never heard of it—that is, until Mr. Willoughby asked me about it."

"Wilson."

"Right, Wilson," says the landlord. "Hold on." He closes the door. A few moments later, he opens it again and jangles a set of keys in his hand. "Up we go."

You follow him up a flight of stairs, and he unlocks an office. "Not sure what you'll find," says the landlord.

You look around the room and notice the table and chairs, as described by Mr. Wilson. There is no other furniture, not even a scrap of paper.

"Do you know where I can find the man who rented this room?" you ask.

The landlord scratches his head. "Can't say as I can."

"Do you remember him?"

"Oh, yes. Your Mr. Willoughby, he said the man called himself Duncan Roth."

You sigh. "Ross."

"Yes, yes, Ross. I never got the chap's name myself.

His rent money spoke loud enough that I never thought to ask." He laughs at himself. "But now I'm thinking, he did like to go to the Rusty Nail. That's the pub across from here." He leads you to the window and points to a building across the street.

You thank the landlord for his help and cross over to the Rusty Nail. As you step inside, your eyes take a moment to adjust to the darkness. You wrinkle your nose; the room smells like rotten potatoes. A small man with red hair is sitting at a table near the back of the pub. Could this be "Duncan Ross"?

You walk toward him, and he looks up at you. His eyes narrow. Then, suddenly, he leaps to his feet. His chair tumbles backward with a clatter, and he darts for the back hallway.

You run after him. You enter the hallway and see a door slamming closed. You yank it open, hurry through it and find yourself in the alley behind the pub. The sun doesn't reach here, and the shadows are stifling. To the right, you catch a glimpse of red hair. The chase is on.

You follow Mr. Ross through a maze of alleys. He manages to stay just ahead.

Panting, you stop to catch your breath and to get your bearings. You are not certain where you are.

You hear a scuffling sound behind you. You turn in time to see Duncan Ross barrelling toward you. But before you can react, his strong hands roughly shove you through an open doorway.

You tumble down a rickety flight of stairs, feeling sharp stabs of pain with every turn. Your aching body slides into a cellar as dark as night. Above you, you hear the door slam and a lock slide into place.

You are trapped, and your body lies broken. Worse yet, it will be days, even weeks before anyone finds you here. By then, it will be too late. Your attempt to solve the Case of the Red-headed League has failed.

**Turn to page 68.**

"These are daring men," you whisper. "Although we shall surprise them, they may harm us unless we are careful. I shall stand behind this crate, and you hide behind those. When I flash a light upon them, we must close in swiftly."

The lights are extinguished, leaving you in total darkness—such an absolute darkness as you have never experienced before. There is something sad and lonely in the gloom and in the cold dank air of the vault.

"They have just one retreat," you add. "Back through the house into Coburg Square. I hope you have done what I asked, Jones."

"I have an inspector and two officers waiting at the front door," he tells you.

"Then we have stopped all the holes. And now we must be silent and wait."

**Go to the next page.**

# The Trap Is Sprung

How long has it been? Certainly more than an hour. Your limbs are weary and stiff. Your nerves are worked up to the highest pitch of tension. Your hearing is so focused that you can hear the gentle breathing of your companions.

Your eyes catch the glint of a light in the direction of the floor. At first it is but a spark upon the pavement. It lengthens out until it becomes a yellow line. Then, without any warning or sound, a gash seems to open in the stone. A hand appears. It feels around for a moment and is withdrawn quickly. All is dark again except the single spark, which marks a chink between the stones.

With a tearing sound, one of the white floor stones turns over upon its side. It leaves a square, gaping hole, and through it streams the light of a lantern. A boyish face peeps up over the edge. The young man looks around, and then he lifts himself shoulder-high and waist-high, until one knee rests upon the edge. In another instant he stands at the side of the hole. He turns and hauls up his companion, thin and small like himself, with a pale face and very red hair.

"It's all clear," he whispers.

The time is now. You must make your move.

If you have a club, turn to page 62.

If you have a gun, turn to page 9.

If you have a knife, turn to page 52.

You casually cross the room to your desk. You open the top drawer as if you're looking for a piece of paper. Instead, you reach inside and remove a revolver. You point it at Mr. Wilson. "While your story is an amusing one, Mr. Wilson, I cannot take it seriously."

Watson nods his approval.

Mr. Wilson's eyes narrow, darting from you to the revolver. "What is this about?" he exclaims. "Are you calling me a liar?"

"Of course not," you reply coolly. "However, I admit that I expected more from you, Professor Moriarty, than a half-baked tale of a ridiculous Red-headed League."

Mr. Wilson's face turns as red as his hair. His cheeks puff out in anger. "Who is Moriarty?" he blusters. "What are you getting at, Holmes?"

"You, sir, are under arrest," you announce.

**Go to the next page.**

You and Dr. Watson escort Mr. Wilson to the police station. There, you explain that he is Professor Moriarty and that he has been scheming to ruin you for years.

The officer at the front desk stares at you confused. Then he looks at Mr. Wilson and says, "Jabez, what's this all about?"

You feel the blood drain from your face. "You know this man?" you ask.

"Of course," replies the policeman. "He's the pawn-broker from Coburg Square."

With a shaking hand, you lower your revolver.

Mr. Wilson levels you with a stare that could melt an icicle. "Mark my words, Holmes. You will never work as a detective again."

The next day, you open the newspaper. You find your mistake splashed across the front page: CONSULTING DETECTIVE ARRESTS INNOCENT MAN.

Weeks pass without a single client or case. Soon, the day comes when you can no longer justify your sign, "Sherlock Holmes, Consulting Detective."

Watson strolls up the street just as you remove the sign. He breaks into a hurried jog. "Holmes! What are you doing?" he asks, huffing for breath.

You hold the sign in your hands, running your lean fingers over the letters. "One can no longer call himself a detective if there are no clients who wish him to detect," you say.

You put your hand on your friend's shoulder. "Thank you, Watson. It has been intriguing, to say the least."

You give him a sad smile and pat his shoulder. There is nothing more to say. Sherlock Holmes, Consulting Detective, is out of business.

**Turn to page 68.**

You pause for a moment, deep in thought. Then you look at Watson and smile, a decision made.

"I would like to hear more from Mr. Jabez Wilson. Please call on him so that we may meet."

Watson nods. "I will do as you ask." He starts away but stops himself. He turns back toward you and adds, "Holmes, be careful."

**Go to the next page.**

You stand inside your office, locked in conversation with Mr. Jabez Wilson. He is a stout, elderly gentleman with fiery red hair. Your friend Dr. Watson steps into the room to join you. Mr. Wilson half rises from his chair and gives a bob of greeting.

You fall into your armchair, putting your fingertips together. "Mr. Wilson has begun sharing one of the most interesting tales I have heard in quite some time," you tell your friend. "Perhaps, Mr. Wilson, you would start again. Dr. Watson has not heard the opening, and the peculiar story makes me anxious to memorize every last detail."

Your client puffs out his chest with pride. He pulls a wrinkled newspaper from the inside pocket of his coat. He glances down at the advertisement column with his head thrust forward. But he stops and looks up, as if an idea has just now occurred to him.

"Before I continue, Mr. Holmes, may I ask you to prove your abilities as a detective? This matter is of great importance to me. I wish only to work with the best."

You nod your approval. "And what do you have in mind, Mr. Wilson?"

"Only a small test. I wish for you to tell something of me, simply by my appearance."

You respond with laughter.

"It is a simple wish," you agree. "Let me begin with your hands, my dear sir. Your right hand is quite a size larger than your left."

"What do you suggest this means?" he asks.

If this reveals to you that Mr. Wilson is (or has been) ill, turn to page 56.

If this reveals to you that Mr. Wilson is (or has been) a hard worker, turn to page 33.

"Of course, the pin can mean only one thing. You are obviously an airplane pilot," you announce.

"Air what?" blusters Mr. Wilson.

You shake your head in confusion, not sure where these crazy words came from. It is 1890, after all. There is no such thing as an airplane.

You see a brief image in your mind: a giant, metal tube with wings hurling through the sky. You wonder if you're going mad. Watson stares at you as if daisies have suddenly sprouted from your head.

Mr. Wilson's face turns as red as his hair. He stands and points at you with a shaking finger. "You're making fun of me with nonsense words. You, sir, are a fraud!"

He stomps toward the door. He pushes past Watson and then turns back to you. "Everyone will hear of your fraud, Sherlock Holmes. Everyone!"

The door slams behind him. You and Dr. Watson are left in a stunned and awkward silence.

Finally Watson clears his throat. "Well, Holmes, I expect we haven't heard the last of Mr. Jabez Wilson."

**Turn to page 67.**

You must now choose a weapon to bring with you on tonight's adventure. Select one of the following:

**Club:** For hand-to-hand combat, a club is a very good choice. It is not intimidating, but it gets the job done. Of course, if your adversary has a more deadly weapon, you may be in trouble.

**Gun:** This weapon will do you little good in close quarters, but it is perfect for halting a fleeing criminal. And there is no weapon better for stopping a criminal from attacking.

**Knife:** If you get into a tussle, a knife is a good weapon to have. It will ensure that the fight is a short one, although it may leave your adversary more injured than you intend.

**After you select your weapon, turn to page 12.**

"Well done, Holmes, as always," Watson exclaims, clapping you on the back. "What shall be your next move, my friend?"

To take Mr. Wilson's case, turn to page 46.

To take Miss Stoner's case, turn to page 72.

To take Mr. Rairy's case, turn to page 88.

If you've finished all three cases, turn to page 152.

You spring out and grab the intruder by the collar.

"Great Scott! Jump, Archie, jump," he shouts.

The other man dives down the hole. You hear the sound of tearing cloth as Jones clutches at his jacket.

The light flashes upon the barrel of a revolver, but your knife comes down on the man's hand, and the pistol clinks upon the stone floor.

"It's no use, John Clay," you tell him. "You have no chance at all."

"So I see," he answers with coolness. "But my pal has escaped, although I see you have a piece of his coat."

"Three men are waiting for him at the door," you tell the criminal.

"Oh, indeed! You have done the thing completely. I must compliment you."

"And I you," you answer. "Your red-headed idea was very new and effective."

"Mr. Clay, you'll see your partner again presently," says Mr. Jones. "Now, would you please march upstairs, where we can get you to the police station?"

John Clay makes a sweeping bow to you and then walks quietly off in the custody of the detective.

"Really, Mr. Holmes," says Mr. Merryweather, "I do not know how the bank can thank you or repay you. There is no doubt that you have defeated one of the most determined attempts at robbery that has ever come."

"I am repaid by having had an experience which is unique," you reply, "and by hearing the very remarkable narrative of the Red-headed League."

**Go to the next page.**

In the early hours of morning, you sit with Watson over a glass of soda at your office on Baker Street.

"You see, Watson," you explain, "the only possible object of the League must be to get the pawnbroker out of the way for a number of hours every day. It was a very curious way of managing it, but it would be difficult to suggest a better. They put in the ad and managed to arrange his absence every morning of the week. From the time I heard of the assistant coming for half wages, it was obvious that he had some strong motive."

"How could you guess the motive?" Watson asks.

"The man's business was small. There was nothing in his house worthy of such preparations, so it must be something out of the house. What could it be? I thought of the assistant's fondness for photography and his trick of vanishing into the cellar. The cellar! There was the end of this tangled clue. He was doing something in the cellar which took many hours a day. What could it be? I could only think that he was digging a tunnel to some other building.

"We went to visit the scene, and I surprised you by beating the pavement with my stick. I was determining whether the cellar stretched out in front or behind. It was not in front. Then I rang the bell. As I hoped, the assistant answered. I hardly looked at his face. His knees were what I wished to see. You must yourself have remarked how worn and stained they were. They were evidence of his many hours of burrowing. The only remaining point was what they were burrowing for. I walked around the corner, saw the bank behind our friend's place, and felt that I had solved my problem. I called upon Scotland Yard and upon the chairman of the bank directors, with the result that you have seen."

"How could you tell they would make their attempt tonight?" Watson asks.

"When they closed their League offices, that was a sign that they cared no longer about Mr. Wilson. In other words, they had completed their tunnel. It was essential that they use it soon, as it might be discovered. Saturday would suit them better than any other day, as it would give them two days for their escape. For all of these reasons I expected them to come tonight."

**Turn to page 51.**

You shake your head with a grin. "An obvious fact, sir. At some point in your childhood, you caught a disease which caused a lack of muscle development in your left hand."

Mr. Wilson's eyes go wide. His face turns as red as his hair. He stands and points at you with a shaking finger. "You, sir, are a fraud!"

You and Watson look at each other in shock. You sit up in your chair, gripping the armrests. "Explain your accusation, Mr. Wilson," you say calmly.

Mr. Wilson holds up his right hand and makes a fist. "This hand is larger because it is stronger. I began my career as a ship's carpenter, and I am right-handed."

He stomps toward the door. He pushes past Watson and then turns back to you. "Everyone will hear of your fraud, Sherlock Holmes. Everyone!"

The door slams behind him. You and Dr. Watson are left in a stunned and awkward silence.

Finally Watson clears his throat. "Well, Holmes, I expect we haven't heard the last of Mr. Jabez Wilson."

**Turn to page 67.**

You smile at Dr. Watson and say, "Mr. Wilson's experience has been a most entertaining one. I believe him." You turn toward your client. "I wouldn't miss your case for the world. It is most unusual. But there is something just a little funny about it. What steps did you take when you found the card upon the door?"

"I went to the building's landlord, and I asked him if he could tell me what had become of the Red-headed League. He said that he had never heard of any such thing. Then I asked him who Mr. Duncan Ross was. He answered that the name was new to him. It would seem, sir, that no one has ever heard of Duncan Ross."

"Your case is remarkable," you assure Mr. Wilson. "I shall be happy to look into it."

"I want to find out about them, and who they are, and what their object was in playing this prank upon me," says Mr. Wilson.

"We shall clear up these points for you. But first, one or two questions, Mr. Wilson. This assistant of yours, how long had he been with you before you learned of the Red-headed League?"

"About a month."

"How did he come?"

"In answer to an advertisement."

"Why did you hire him?"

"Because he was handy and would come cheap."

"What is he like, this Vincent Spaulding?"

"Small, stout, very quick in his ways. He has no hair on his face, but he's over thirty years old. He also has a white splash of acid on his forehead."

You sit up in your chair in excitement. "I thought as much. Have you observed that his ears are pierced?"

"Yes, sir. He told me that a gypsy had done it for him when he was a lad."

You sink back into your chair. "Has your business been attended to in your absence?"

"Nothing to complain of, sir. There's never much to do in the morning."

"Thank you, Mr. Wilson. I shall be happy to give you an opinion on the subject in a day or two. Today is Saturday. I hope that by Monday we will have this case solved."

"Well, Watson," you say when your visitor has left, "what do you make of it all?"

"It is a most mysterious business," he answers.

"As a rule," you remind him, "the more bizarre a thing is, the less mysterious it proves to be."

"What are you going to do?" he asks.

You curl yourself up in your chair, your knees drawn to your nose. You close your eyes and think about the clues you have just been given. It would benefit you to find the man who called himself Duncan Ross. He will certainly provide answers to this mystery. Yet you also wonder if Mr. Wilson's assistant, Vincent Spaulding, plays a more important role in this scheme.

You must decide. Will you spend the day tracking down Duncan Ross? Or will you investigate Vincent Spaulding? What will you choose to do?

To look for Duncan Ross, turn to page 36.

To find Vincent Spaulding, turn to page 29.

A league of red-heads? A woman afraid for her life two years after her sister's death? An important military man with a tale of sabotage? They all sound like traps to you.

"Watson," you declare, "we shall not be taking any of these cases. Moriarty is behind each and every one, I assure you."

Watson nods thoughtfully. "I think you are making a wise choice, Holmes."

Over the next few weeks, each case that presents itself sounds like one of Moriarty's clever traps. You turn them all down: a mysterious death in Boscombe Valley, a bride who disappears on her wedding day, a countess's lost jewel, and more.

You keep your shutters closed, and you constantly pace in the dim recesses of your office. Fewer and fewer requests come your way. Finally, the day arrives when you can no longer justify your sign, "Sherlock Holmes, Consulting Detective."

Watson strolls up the street just as you remove the sign. He breaks into a hurried jog.

"Holmes! What are you doing?" he asks, huffing to catch his breath.

You hold the sign in your hands, running your lean fingers over the letters. "One can no longer call himself a detective if there are no clients who wish him to detect," you say.

You put your hand on your friend's shoulder. "Thank you, Watson. It has been intriguing, to say the least."

You give him a sad smile and pat his shoulder. There is nothing more to say. Sherlock Holmes, Consulting Detective, is out of business.

**Turn to page 68.**

You spring out and grab the intruder by the collar.

"Great Scott! Jump, Archie, jump," he shouts.

The other man dives down the hole. You hear the sound of tearing cloth as Jones clutches at his jacket.

The light flashes upon the barrel of a revolver, but your club comes down on the man's wrist, and the pistol clinks upon the stone floor.

"It's no use, John Clay," you tell him. "You have no chance at all."

"So I see," he answers with coolness. "But my pal has escaped, although I see you have a piece of his coat."

"Three men are waiting for him at the door," you tell the criminal.

"Oh, indeed! You have done the thing completely. I must compliment you."

"And I you," you answer. "Your red-headed idea was very new and effective."

"Mr. Clay, you'll see your partner again presently," says Mr. Jones. "Now, would you please march upstairs, where we can get you to the police station?"

John Clay makes a sweeping bow to you and then walks quietly off in the custody of the detective.

"Really, Mr. Holmes," says Mr. Merryweather, "I do not know how the bank can thank you or repay you. There is no doubt that you have defeated one of the most determined attempts at robbery that has ever come."

"I am repaid by having had an experience which is unique," you reply, "and by hearing the very remarkable narrative of the Red-headed League."

**Turn to the page 54.**

"These are daring men," you whisper. "We must be swift in nabbing them. We shall stand right here."

The four of you arrange yourselves around the spot you believe John Clay will enter.

The lights are extinguished, leaving you in total darkness—such an absolute darkness as you have never experienced before. There is something sad and lonely in the gloom and in the cold dank air of the vault.

"They have just one retreat," you add. "Back through the house into Coburg Square. I hope you have done what I asked, Jones."

"I have an inspector and two officers waiting at the front door," he tells you.

"Then we have stopped all the holes. And now we must be silent and wait."

**Go to the next page.**

# The Trap Is Sprung

How long has it been? Certainly more than an hour. Your limbs are weary and stiff. Your nerves are worked to the highest pitch of tension. You can hear the gentle breathing of your companions.

Your eyes catch the glint of a light in the direction of the floor. At first it is but a spark upon the pavement. It lengthens out until it becomes a yellow line. Then, without any warning or sound, a gash seems to open in the stone. A hand appears. It feels around for a moment and is withdrawn quickly. All is dark again except the single spark, which marks a chink between the stones.

With a tearing sound, one of the white floor stones turns over upon its side. It leaves a square, gaping hole, through which streams the light of a lantern. A boyish face peeps up over the edge. His eyes widen in surprise. He calls into the tunnel behind him. He has spotted you too soon.

You lunge forward and grab John Clay's coat. The villain smiles coldly. In a flash of motion, he reaches backward and grabs a large shovel. He swings it toward your head. You hear a thunder-like clap, and you feel a sharp, piercing pain. You crumple to the ground, and then you know no more.

**Turn to page 68.**

Over the next several weeks, your business slows. Fewer and fewer people come to you for help. Finally the day arrives when you can no longer justify your sign, "Sherlock Holmes, Consulting Detective."

Watson strolls up the street just as you remove the sign. He breaks into a hurried jog. "Holmes! What are you doing?" he asks, huffing for breath.

You hold the sign in your hands, running your lean fingers over the letters. "One can no longer call himself a detective if there are no clients who wish him to detect," you say.

You put your hand on your friend's shoulder. "Thank you, Watson. It has been intriguing, to say the least."

You give him a sad smile and pat his shoulder. There is nothing more to say. Sherlock Holmes, Consulting Detective, is out of business.

**Go to the next page.**

# The End

## Try Again

You hesitate for a moment, weighing your options. As the sound grows fainter, you decide that the risk is too great. You step away from the book and creep carefully back the way you came.

By the time you reach the entrance, the adventurous noise is gone. You slowly climb out of the attic and slide the panel into place above you. You hurry to your homework, confident that you have done the right thing. After all, if you fail one more math assignment, you're pretty sure you'll be grounded for life.

Nevertheless, as you retake your seat at the desk, you can't help but wonder if you've missed a rare opportunity, one that might have changed your life forever.

"Oh, well," you tell yourself. "It's too late to think about that now."

You grab your pencil and dive once more into the word problem that has stumped you. The solution does not come, but that's okay. You can guess. If you get it wrong, well, there's always summer school.

**Turn to page 68.**

You grab your knife from the pocket of your coat and wave it at Colonel Rairy. "The only thing we shall be examining is how your plan failed."

Watson rushes to your side. "What are you doing, Holmes?" he exclaims.

"Do you care to explain, or shall I?" you ask Rairy.

A wide grin spreads slowly across his face. With one swift move, he turns and follows his female companion through the door.

A moment later, he reappears, holding a revolver. You suddenly find yourself looking straight down the barrel of a gun.

"Drop your weapon," says Rairy.

Reluctantly, you let the knife clatter to the floor.

"I don't understand," says Watson. "What's all this about, Holmes?"

You keep your voice steady and calm. "Our client is actually the famed Professor Moriarty."

"Well done, Holmes," says the villain. "You reasoned it out. I wish I could be as quick and clever as you." He steps back in mock surprise, holding a hand to his chest. "Oh, wait, I am!"

Moriarty inclines his head toward the door, keeping the revolver pointed straight at you. "Move it."

You and Watson are forced outside and into the night's darkness. Your life is at an end, and you know it. You can imagine the coming newspaper headline: FAMED DETECTIVE MISSING, WORST FEARED.

Indeed, it is the worst. You are Sherlock Holmes, Consulting Detective, and because you chose poorly, you will never be heard from again.

**Turn to page 68.**

You hesitate before making up your mind. Then you nod at your friend and smile. "I would like to hear more from Miss Helen Stoner. Her case sounds dire."

Watson scowls. "Are you sure, Holmes?"

"Oh, Watson, don't be silly. Yes, of course, I am sure. Please call for her."

"Very well." He shakes his head and starts away, but he stops himself. He turns back toward you and adds, "Holmes, be careful."

**Go to the next page.**

You accompany your friend to the sitting room. A lady dressed in black, and sitting by the window, rises as you enter.

"Good day, madam," you say cheerily. "My name is Sherlock Holmes. This is my friend, Watson. Before we begin, I shall get you a cup of hot coffee, for I observe that you are shivering."

"It is not cold which makes me shiver," she says.

"What, then?" you ask.

"It is fear, Mr. Holmes. It is terror."

As she speaks, you can see that she is upset. Her face is drawn and gray with frightened eyes, like those of some hunted animal. Her features are those of a woman of 30, but her hair is peppered with gray. Her expression is a very tired one.

"You must not fear," you tell her, patting her arm. "We shall soon set matters right. I have no doubt."

"Sir, I can stand this no longer. I shall go mad if it continues. I have no one to turn to. I have heard of you, Mr. Holmes. Oh, do you think you could help me?"

"I shall devote the same care to your case as I do to all of my cases. Now will you tell us about the matter?"

"Alas!" replies your visitor. "The true horror of my situation lies in the fact that my fears are vague. My suspicions depend upon small points, which will not seem important to another. However, I have heard, Mr. Holmes, that you can see into the wickedness of the human heart. You may advise me how to survive these dangers."

"I am all attention, madam."

**Go to the next page.**

# The Speckled Band

"My name is Helen Stoner, and I am living with my stepfather, Dr. Roylott."

You nod your head. "The name is familiar to me."

"The family was at one time among the richest in all of England. In the last century, however, most of their money was lost. Nothing was left but a few acres and the 200-year-old house. My stepfather took a loan from a relative, which allowed him to earn a medical degree. He went out to India and established a large practice. In a fit of anger, however, he hurt his native butler. He was sent to prison. Afterwards, he returned to England.

"When Dr. Roylott was in India, he married my mother, the young widow of Major-General Stoner.

My sister Julia and I were twins. My mother was rich. When she died in a train accident, Dr. Roylott took us to live with him in the old house at Stoke Moran. My mother's money was enough for all our wants, but a terrible change came over our stepfather. He shut himself up in his house and seldom came out. He grew violent and became the terror of the village. Folks would flee at his approach, for he is a man of great strength and even greater anger."

**Go to the next page.**

"Pardon me, Mr. Holmes," says Miss Stoner. "But before I go on, may I ask for proof of your detective skills? My very life may be at stake; I must work with someone who can truly help me."

You nod in approval. "What will you have me do?"

"Are you able to tell something about how I arrived here this morning?"

You smile confidently. "I observe the second half of a return ticket in the palm of your left glove."

"And what does this tell you?" she asks.

If you believe this means that Miss Stoner arrived by bus, turn to page 100.

If you believe this means that Miss Stoner arrived by train, turn to page 120.

Dr. Roylott bends the metal poker into a curve with his huge hands. "See that you keep yourself out of my grip," he snarls. Then he hurls the twisted poker into the fireplace and strides out of the room.

"He seems a very friendly person," you say, laughing. "This incident gives zest to our investigation. I only hope that Miss Stoner will not suffer for allowing this brute to follow her."

**Go to the next page.**

It is after one o'clock when you return from your errands. You hold in your hand a sheet of blue paper, written over with notes and figures.

"I have seen the will of the deceased wife," you tell Watson. "The total inheritance is $250,000. Each daughter can claim $100,000 once married. It is evident, therefore, that if both girls had married, Dr. Roylott would lose most of that money. It has proven that he has motives for standing in the way of anything of the sort. And now, Watson, we shall call a cab and drive to Waterloo."

At Waterloo, you catch a train for Leatherhead. There, you hire a carriage and ride for four or five miles through the Surrey lanes. You sit in front, your arms folded, your hat pulled down over your eyes. You are buried in deep thought, your chin upon your chest.

"Look there," says Watson.

A tree-filled park stretches up in a slope, thickening into a grove at the highest point. From amid the trees there juts out the roof of a very old mansion.

"Stoke Moran?" you ask your driver.

"Yes, that be the house of Dr. Grimesby Roylott."

"That is where we are going," you say.

"There's the village," says the driver, pointing to a cluster of roofs some distance to the left. "But if you want to get to the house, you'll find it shorter to go by the foot-path over the fields. There it is, where the lady is walking."

"And the lady is Miss Stoner," you observe. "Yes, I think we had better do as you suggest."

You hop off the carriage, pay your fare and start toward Miss Stoner.

Your client hurries to meet you. "I have been waiting so eagerly for you," she cries. "Dr. Roylott has gone to town. It is unlikely he will be back before evening."

"We have already met the doctor," you say and, in a few words, explain what occurred.

Miss Stoner turns white to the lips. "Good heavens! He is so cunning that I never know when I am safe from him. What will he say when he returns?"

"He must guard himself, for he may find that there is someone more cunning than he. Lock yourself up from him tonight. If he is violent, we shall take you away to your aunt's. Now, we must make the best use of our time."

It is up to you to quickly piece together this mystery. A woman's life depends upon it. To do so, you must first decide where to look for clues. Does the solution to this case lie with the gypsies? Or will you find your answers at the scene of the crime? Which should you investigate? What will you choose to do?

To investigate the bedrooms, turn to page 93.

To investigate the gypsies, turn to page 124.

You smile at Watson and remark, "Don't worry, old friend. I believe him."

You go upstairs together, Colonel Rairy first with the lamp, you and Watson behind him. It is a maze of an old house, with corridors, passages, narrow winding staircases, and little low doors. There are no carpets and no signs of any furniture above the ground floor.

Your client stops at last before a door and unlocks it. Within it is a small, square room. The three of you can hardly fit into it at one time.

"We are now," says Rairy, "within the hydraulic press. It would be an unpleasant thing if anyone were to turn it on. The ceiling of this chamber is really the end of the descending piston. It comes down with the force of many tons upon this metal floor. Perhaps you will have the goodness to look around, Mr. Holmes, and to see if you might find any clues."

You take the lamp from the colonel and examine the machine very thoroughly. It is indeed a large one and capable of pushing down with enormous pressure.

**Go to the next page.**

An examination shows that one of the bands, which is around the head of a driving-rod, has been cut. This is clearly the cause of the loss of power.

You point it out to your client, who follows your remarks carefully. He asks several practical questions as to how they should set it right. As you explain yourself, he mends the problem right before your eyes.

"Your suspect is quite obviously someone who knows the workings of this machinery," you add. "Is there anyone else whom I might be able to interview?"

Colonel Rairy's face sets hard, and a wicked light springs up in his grey eyes. He takes a step backward and says, "Goodbye, Sherlock Holmes. I thought you were a worthy adversary. I was, however, mistaken." He slams the little door and turns the key in the lock.

You rush toward it and pull at the handle, but it is secure. It does not give in to your kicks and shoves.

"Forgive me, Watson," you say to your friend. "We have been tricked."

You suddenly hear a sound which sends your heart into your mouth. It is the clank of the levers. Rairy has set the engine at work. The black ceiling comes down upon you, slowly, with a force which will soon grind you to a pulp.

You throw yourself against the door and claw with your fingernails at the lock. The remorseless clanking of the levers drowns your cries for help.

The ceiling is only a foot or two above your head. With your hand upraised you can feel its hard, rough surface. Soon, you are unable to stand. A few moments after that, the clang of the two metal slabs marks the end of Watson and the end of you.

**Turn to page 68.**

You must now choose a weapon to bring with you on tonight's adventure. Select one of the following:

**Club:** For hand-to-hand combat, a club is a very good choice. It is not intimidating, but it gets the job done. Of course, if your adversary has a more deadly weapon, you may be in trouble.

**Gun:** This weapon will do you little good in close quarters, but it is perfect for halting a fleeing criminal. And there is no weapon better for stopping a criminal from attacking.

**Knife:** If you get into a tussle, a knife is a good weapon to have. It will ensure that the fight is a short one, although it may leave your adversary more injured than you intend.

**After you select your weapon, turn to page 103.**

You break into a low laugh. "That is the baboon," you murmur to your friend.

You slip off your shoes and climb into the bedroom. You noiselessly close the shutters, move the lamp onto the table, and cast your eyes round the room. All is as you had seen it in the daytime.

You creep up to Watson and whisper, "The least sound would be fatal to our plans. We must sit without light. He would see it through the ventilator."

Watson nods.

"Do not go asleep," you add. "Your very life may depend upon it. I will sit on the side of the bed, and you in that chair. Remain perfectly alert."

You place your weapon upon the bed beside you, along with a box of matches and the stump of a candle. Then you turn down the lamp and are left in darkness. You cannot hear a sound, not even the drawing of a breath. You rest in a state of nervous tension.

From outside comes the occasional cry of a night-bird. Once, at your window, a long catlike whine tells you that the cheetah is roaming. The clock strikes twelve and one and two and three. Still you sit, waiting.

Suddenly, there is the gleam of a light up in the ventilator. It vanishes but is followed by a strong smell of burning oil and heated metal. Someone in the next room has lit a dark-lantern. You hear a gentle sound of movement, and then all is silent once more.

For half an hour you sit with straining ears. Then another sound becomes audible: a gentle, soothing sound, like a small jet of steam escaping from a kettle. The instant you hear it, you spring from the bed, strike a match, and grab your weapon.

If you have a club, turn to page 145.

If you have a gun, turn to page 101.

If you have a knife, turn to page 141.

You gaze out the window, deep in thought. At last, you turn to your friend and smile. "Mr. Rairy may very well be an important man. Let's not keep him waiting any longer."

Watson nods in agreement. "I shall find him straight away, Holmes, and I believe he is a colonel." He starts away but pauses at the door. He turns back to you and says, "Holmes, be careful."

**Go to the next page.**

You enter your sitting-room and find a gentleman seated there. He wears a thick, shaggy beard and large glasses. He is quietly dressed in a suit, with a cloth cap laid down upon your books. You receive him in your quietly polite fashion, order fresh ham, and join him in a hearty meal.

When it is concluded, you seat your acquaintance upon the sofa and set a glass of water within his reach. "Please, tell us how we might assist you, Colonel Rairy," you say.

He nods. "I wish to take little of your time, so I shall start at once."

You sit in your big armchair with a weary expression that hides your keen and eager nature. Dr. Watson sits opposite to you, and you listen to your visitor's story.

"You have been recommended to me, Mr. Holmes, as a man who is great at his profession and who is also capable of keeping a secret."

You bow. "May I ask who gave such a good reference?"

"Perhaps it is better that I should not tell. But I will say that my work is very important and top secret. You might even call it a matter of national security. I have an assignment for you, but absolute secrecy is a must. Absolute secrecy, you understand."

"You may depend on my silence," you assure him.

He looks hard at you. "Do you promise, then?"

"Yes, I promise."

"Very good," he says. "I require your opinion about a hydraulic machine which presses metal into bricks for the military. The machine has been tampered with. If you can guess who sabotaged it, we shall set matters right. What do you think of such an assignment?"

"It sounds fine," you tell him. "But I assure you, there will be no guessing on my part."

"Excellent," says he. "We shall want you to come tonight by the last train."

"Where to?"

"To Eyford, within seven miles of Reading. There is a train which would bring you there at about 11:15."

"Very good," you say.

"I shall come down in a carriage to meet you."

"There is a drive, then?" you ask.

"Yes, our little place is quite out in the country. It is a good seven miles from Eyford Station."

"That is very awkward. Could I not come at some earlier hour?"

"We have judged it best that you should come late. Still, of course, if you would like to back out of this business, there is plenty of time to do so."

You must admit: The case is vague and mysterious. Could this be Professor Moriarty's trap? If so, it is best to decline the case. However, he said his problem is a matter of national security. If you decline the case, you may be putting all of England at risk. What will you choose to do?

To accept the case, turn to page 116.

To turn down the case, turn to page 129.

"An obvious fact," you reply with confidence. "You walked from the train station this morning, madam. That road is quite muddy."

Miss Stoner's face pales. She draws a deep breath and closes her eyes. When she opens them, they shimmer with tears. "You are a cruel man," she says at last. "For a moment, I had hoped . . ." her voice trails off.

The depth of misery in her eyes and her accusing tone cause you to take a step back.

"You cannot help me," she whispers. "No one can." She exits so quickly that it is almost as if she was never there at all.

You stand rooted to your spot, staring numbly at the vacant place where Miss Stoner used to be.

**Turn to page 67.**

# A Puzzling Crime Scene

"Kindly take us to the bedrooms we are to examine," you request.

The building is of gray stone, with a high central portion and two curving wings on each side. In one of these wings, the windows are broken and blocked with wooden boards, while the roof is partly caved in. The central portion is in little better repair, but the right-hand block appears modern. The blinds in the windows, with smoke curling up from the chimneys, show that this is where the family lives.

You walk slowly up and down the ill-trimmed lawn. You examine with deep attention the outsides of the bedroom windows.

"This, I take it, belongs to the room where you used to sleep. The center one was your sister's, and the one next to the main building was Dr. Roylott's."

"Exactly, but I am now sleeping in the middle one."

"There does not seem to be any need for repairs at your old room," you note.

"There were none. I believe that it was an excuse to move me from my room."

"Ah! That is suggestive. Now, on the other side of this narrow wing runs the corridor from which these three rooms open. There are windows in it, of course?"

"Yes, but too narrow for anyone to pass through."

"You both locked your doors at night, so your rooms were unapproachable from that side. Would you have the kindness to go into your room and bar your shutters?"

Miss Stoner does so, and you try in every way to force the shutter open, but without success. There is no way to raise the bar. With your lens, you test the hinges, but they are of solid iron.

"Hum," you say, scratching your chin. "No one could pass through these shutters if they were bolted. Well, we shall see if the inside throws any light upon the matter."

A side door leads into the corridor. You proceed to the second bedroom, in which Miss Stoner now sleeps and in which her sister met her fate. It is a quaint little room, with a low ceiling and a gaping fireplace. A brown chest of drawers stands in one corner, a narrow bed in another, and a dressing table on the left-hand side of the window. These articles, with two small chairs, make up all the furniture in the room. The walls are of brown, worm-eaten oak.

You pull one of the chairs into a corner and sit. Your eyes travel round and round and up and down, taking in every detail of the room.

"Where does that bell communicate to?" you ask. You point to a thick bell-rope which hangs down beside the bed. The end actually lies upon the pillow.

"To the housekeeper's room," says Miss Stoner.

"It looks newer than the other things."

"Yes, it was only put there a couple of years ago," your client replies.

"Your sister asked for it, I suppose?"

"No, I never heard of her using it. We used to always get what we wanted for ourselves."

"Then it seems odd to put so nice a bell-pull there. You will excuse me for a few minutes." You throw yourself down upon your face. With your lens in hand, you crawl swiftly backward and forward, examining the cracks between the boards. Then you do the same with the woodwork.

You walk to the bed and spend some time staring at it. You run your eye up and down the wall. Finally you take the bell-rope in your hand and give it a brisk tug.

"Why, it's a dummy," you say, surprised.

"Won't it ring?" asks Miss Stoner.

"No, it is not even attached to a wire. Interesting, I can see now that it is fastened to a hook just above where the little opening for the ventilator is."

"How strange," says Miss Stoner. "I never noticed that before."

"Very strange indeed," you mutter, pulling at the rope. "There are one or two peculiar points about this room. For example, why does the ventilator open into another room? It should communicate with outside air."

"That is also quite new," says the lady.

"Done the same time as the bell-rope?" you ask.

"Yes, there were several changes about that time."

"Dummy bell-ropes and ventilators which do not really ventilate. With your permission, Miss Stoner, we shall carry our researches into the next room."

Dr. Grimesby Roylott's chamber is larger than that of his stepdaughter but is as plainly furnished: a bed, a small wooden shelf full of books, an armchair beside the bed, a plain wooden chair against the wall, a round table, and a large safe.

You walk slowly around and examine each and all of them with the keenest interest. "What's in here?" you ask, tapping the safe.

"My stepfather's business papers."

"Have you seen inside, then?"

"Only once, some years ago. I remember that it was full of papers."

"There isn't a cat in it, for example?"

"No. What a strange idea!"

"Well, look at this." You pick up a small saucer of milk from atop the safe.

"No, we don't keep a cat. But as I mentioned, there is a cheetah and a baboon."

"Ah, yes, of course. Well, a cheetah is just a big cat, yet a saucer of milk does not go very far in satisfying its wants. There is one point I should wish to determine." You squat in front of the wooden chair and examine the seat with great attention.

"Thank you. That is quite settled," you say, rising and putting your lens in your pocket. "Hello! Here is something interesting!"

The object which catches your eye is a small dog lash hung on one corner of the bed. The lash is curled upon itself and tied so as to make a loop of whipcord.

"What do you make of that, Watson?"

"It's a common enough lash. But I don't know why it should be tied."

"That is not quite so common, is it? It's a wicked world, and when a clever man turns his brains to crime it is the worst of all."

**Go to the next page.**

"There is more I wish to show you," says Miss Stoner. "Will you have time to see it?"

If you are caught by Dr. Roylott, your investigation will be ruined. Miss Stoner will be in more danger than ever. However, she may yet show you the clue which will explain the entire mystery. You cannot save her without first closing this case. What will you choose to do?

To exit the mansion now, turn to page 142.

To investigate more clues, turn to page 131.

"An obvious fact," you reply. "Your ticket could have come from only one place. You arrived by bus."

Miss Stoner's face pales. She draws a deep breath and closes her eyes. When she opens them, they shimmer with tears. "You are a cruel man," she says at last. "For a moment, I had hoped . . ." her voice trails off.

The misery in her eyes and her accusing tone cause you to take a step back.

With a shaking hand, Miss Stoner hands you her ticket stub. "You cannot help me," she whispers. "No one can." She exits so quickly that it is almost as if she was never there at all.

You stand rooted to your spot, staring numbly at the ticket stub from the eight o'clock train.

**Turn to page 67.**

You grab your revolver and point it at the rope. "You see it, Watson?" you yell. "You see it?"

"What, Holmes? What?" replies Watson.

You could end this case in an instant, yet you cannot get a good aim. Your plan is not going well.

You suddenly feel a sharp pain. Before the world fades to black, you realize with dread that the Case of the Speckled Band will be your last.

**Turn to page 68.**

You must now choose a weapon to bring with you on tonight's adventure. Select one of the following:

**Club:** For hand-to-hand combat, a club is a very good choice. It is not intimidating, but it gets the job done. Of course, if your adversary has a more deadly weapon, you may be in trouble.

**Gun:** This weapon will do you little good in close quarters, but it is perfect for halting a fleeing criminal. And there is no weapon better for stopping a criminal from attacking.

**Knife:** If you get into a tussle, a knife is a good weapon to have. It will ensure that the fight is a short one, although it may leave your adversary more injured than you intend.

**After you select your weapon, turn to page 135.**

# Journey into Darkness

You conduct your business for the afternoon, eat a large supper, drive to Paddington, and start off. You and Watson arrive in time for the last train to Eyford, and you reach the dim-lit station after eleven o'clock.

You find your client waiting. Without a word he grasps your arm and hurries you into a carriage. He draws up the windows on either side, taps on the woodwork, and away you move as fast as the horse can go.

You drive for at least an hour. Colonel Rairy sits at your side in silence, looking at you with great intensity. The country roads seem to be in poor condition, for you shake and jolt terribly. You try to look out the windows to see where you are, but they are made of frosted glass.

You can make out nothing more than the occasional bright blur of a passing light.

The bumping of the road is soon exchanged for the crisp smoothness of gravel, and the carriage comes to a stand. Colonel Rairy springs out. You and Watson follow after him.

You step into a dark hall, and the door slams heavily behind you. You hear faintly the rattle of the wheels as the carriage drives away. A door opens at the other end of the passage, and a long, golden bar of light shoots out in your direction. It grows broader, and a woman appears with a lamp in her hand. She holds it above her head, pushing her face forward and peering at you.

She speaks a few words in a foreign language, in a tone as though asking a question. Colonel Rairy says something in her ear, and she returns into the room.

He walks toward you again with a lamp held in his hand. "Perhaps we had better proceed to business. I will take you to see the machine. This is where we compress metal into bricks. We wish you to examine the machine, let us know what is wrong with it, and how someone might have sabotaged it."

At that very moment, your friend Watson leans over and whispers into your ear. "I sense a trap. Our lives may be in peril, Holmes."

You cannot help but agree. Could this be the trap set by Moriarty? Should you arrest this man at once? If you do, you will either be saving yourself from danger or putting all of England in jeopardy. What will you choose to do?

To arrest Tom Rairy, turn to page 119.

To continue with the case, turn to page 82.

There is a long silence. You lean your chin upon your hands and stare into the crackling fire. "I believe you," you say at last. "There are a thousand details which I should know before we act. Yet we have not a moment to lose. If we come today, would it be possible to see these rooms without the knowledge of your stepfather?"

"As it happens, he spoke of coming into town for some important business. He will probably be away all day. We have a housekeeper now, but I could get her out of the way."

"Excellent. You are not averse to this trip, Watson?"

"By no means," he answers.

"Then we shall both come. What are you going to do yourself, Miss Stoner?"

"I have one or two things which I wish to do now that I am in town," says your new client. "But I shall return by the twelve o'clock train."

"You may expect us early in the afternoon. I also have some small business to attend to."

"I must go," says Miss Stoner. "My heart is lightened already since I have confided my trouble to you. I shall look forward to seeing you again this afternoon." She drops her thick black veil over her face and glides from the room.

"What do you think of it all, Watson?" you ask.

"It seems to be a most sinister business. Yet her sister must have been alone when she met her end."

"What of these nightly whistles, and what of the very peculiar words of the dying woman?"

"I do not know."

"When you combine the ideas of whistles at night, a band of gypsies, the fact that the doctor has interest in preventing his stepdaughter's marriage, the dying reference to a band, and the fact that Miss Helen Stoner heard a metallic clang, there is good ground to think that the mystery points toward the gypsies."

"But what, then, did the gypsies do?"

"I cannot imagine, and it is for that reason we are going to Stoke Moran this day."

**Go to the next page.**

Your door is suddenly dashed open. A huge man appears from behind it. He is so tall that his hat brushes the cross bar of the doorway, and his shoulders seem to span it from side to side. A large face, seared with wrinkles and marked with an evil passion, turns from Watson to you. His deep-set eyes and his thin nose give him the resemblance of a fierce old bird of prey.

"Which of you is Holmes?" he asks.

"My name, sir," you reply quietly.

"I am Dr. Grimesby Roylott, of Stoke Moran."

"Indeed," you say politely. "Please take a seat."

"I will do nothing of the kind. My stepdaughter has been here. I have traced her. What has she been saying to you?" Your new visitor takes a step forward. "I have heard of you before. You are Holmes, the meddler."

You chuckle. "Your conversation is most entertaining. When you go out, close the door behind you."

"I will go when I have said my say!" Dr. Roylott roars. "Don't you dare meddle with my affairs. I am a dangerous man." He steps swiftly forward and seizes a metal poker.

Does he mean to attack you? If so, your only hope is to attack first. He is an angry brute. If he gains the upper hand, it will be the end of you, so you should find a weapon and strike first. However, if his motive is not to attack, you will be committing a crime. It will be the end of your career as Consulting Detective. What will you choose to do?

If you believe Roylott will attack, turn to page 117.

If you believe he will not attack, turn to page 78.

"You must have started early," you say. "And yet you had a good drive in a dog-cart before you reached the train station. The marks are fresh. There is no vehicle but a dog-cart which throws up mud in that way, and then only when you sit on the left-hand side of the driver."

"You are perfectly correct," she says. "I started from home before six this morning."

"Of course," you reply without surprise. "Please, continue your narrative."

"Well, I could not sleep that night. A vague feeling of doom impressed me. The wind was howling outside, and the rain was beating and splashing against the windows. Suddenly, I heard the scream of a terrified woman. I knew that it was my sister. I sprang from my bed and rushed into the corridor. As I opened my door, I seemed to hear a low whistle, just as my sister described. A few moments later, I heard a clanging sound, as if a mass of metal had fallen.

"I ran down the passage. My sister's door was unlocked and moving slowly upon its hinges. I stared at it in horror, not knowing what was about to walk from her room. By the light of the corridor, I saw my sister appear.

Her face was white with terror, her hands groping for help. Her whole figure swayed back and forth. I ran to her and threw my arms around her, but at that moment she fell to the ground. As I bent over her, she shrieked out in a voice which I shall never forget, 'Helen! It was the band! The speckled band!'

"There was something else which she would have said, and she stabbed with her finger in the direction of the doctor's room. But a fresh convulsion seized her. I rushed out, calling loudly for my stepfather. When he reached my sister's side, it was too late. Such was the dreadful end of my beloved sister."

"One moment," you say. "Are you sure about this whistle and metallic sound?"

"It is my strong impression that I heard it. Yet I may possibly have been mistaken."

"Was your sister dressed?"

"No, she was in her night-dress. In her right hand was the charred stump of a match, and in her left a match box."

"Showing that she had struck a light and looked around her room. That is important."

"The police investigated the case. They were unable to find any cause of death. My evidence showed that the door had been locked. The windows were blocked by shutters with broad iron bars, which were also locked. The walls were quite solid, and the flooring was also examined with the same result. It is certain, therefore, that my sister was alone when she met her end. Besides, there were no marks of any violence upon her."

"How about poison?"

"The doctors examined her for it, without success."

"What do you think that she died of, then?"

"It is my belief that she died of pure fear and shock, though I cannot imagine what frightened her."

"I know gypsy people are common to the area. Were there gypsies nearby at the time?"

"Yes, there are nearly always some camping at the edge of our property."

"Ah, and what did you gather from this allusion to a band—a speckled band?"

"Sometimes I have thought that it referred to these very gypsies. She may have been referring to the spotted handkerchiefs which so many of them wear."

You shake your head like a man who is far from being satisfied. "These are very deep waters," you say. "Please go on with your narrative."

**Go to the next page.**

# An Unexpected
# Guest

"Two years have passed since then. A month ago, Percy Armitage did me the honor of asking my hand in marriage. We are to be married in the spring.

"But two days ago, some repairs were started, and my bedroom wall was pierced. I had to move into the room where my sister died and to sleep in the very bed in which she slept. Imagine my terror when, last night, I heard the low whistle which had been the herald of her death. I sprang up and lit the lamp, but nothing was seen in the room. I was too shaken to go to bed again, so I dressed. As soon as it was daylight, I came here with the one object of seeing you."

"You have done wisely," you tell her.

"I say so," whispers Watson. "She is wise enough to trick even you. This is surely a trap set by the villain, Professor Moriarty."

There may be something to Dr. Watson's concern. Miss Stoner's tale is too perfect. It almost seems made up, with every detail chosen to arouse your interest. Could this be the trap? Should you send this woman away? If you do, you will either be rescuing yourself from danger or sentencing the poor girl to a horrible fate. What will you choose to do?

To continue with the case, turn to page 106.

To send Miss Stoner away, turn to page 133.

"Not at all," you say. "I am happy to accommodate myself to your wishes."

Colonel Rairy looks at you with a last, long gaze. Then, snapping hand to forehead in a crisp salute, he hurries from the room.

**Turn to page 85.**

In a flash you launch yourself from your chair. You snatch the metal poker from Dr. Roylott's hand. You whirl around him and land the poker with a sickening thud against the backs of his knees. Dr. Roylott topples to the floor. On the way down, he dashes his head against the edge of your stone fireplace.

The metal poker dangles from your hand. You had not intended to wound the man so seriously. You merely wanted to stop him before he attacked.

Watson stares at you in shock, and then he rushes to the big man's side. Dr. Roylott groans and pushes Watson away with one hand; he holds his other hand to the side of his head. He staggers to his feet and fixes you with a stare. Suddenly he grins, an awful sight.

"I meant what I said, Holmes. I am a dangerous man." He lurches out the door, leaving you and Watson alone in a stunned silence.

Not ten minutes later you hear a knock at the door. You open it to find several policemen. They push past you and survey the scene: the poker, the blood on the fireplace and spattered on the floor.

"I'm sorry, Mr. Holmes, but you're under arrest," says the oldest-looking police officer.

"What are the charges?" you ask calmly.

"Assault and battery, sir."

You nod and walk out the door of your home office, followed by the policemen. It will be a long time, you think sadly, before you return.

"Lock up for me, please, Watson," you say. With one rash decision, Sherlock Holmes, Consulting Detective, is out of business.

**Turn to page 68.**

You have chosen to arrest Colonel Rairy.

If you have a club, turn to page 139.

If you have a gun, turn to page 149.

If you have a knife, turn to page 70.

"An obvious fact," you reply. "You have come in by train this morning."

"You are right, sir," says Miss Stoner. "Please allow me to continue."

"I pray you will," you tell her.

"Dr. Roylott has no friends except for the wandering gypsies, and he allows them to camp upon the few acres of the family estate. He has a passion also for Indian animals, which are sent to him by a correspondent. He has at the moment a cheetah and baboon, which wander freely over his grounds and are feared by the villagers.

"You can imagine that my poor sister Julia and I had no great pleasure in our lives. She was 30 at the time of her death, and yet her hair had already begun to whiten, even as mine has."

"Your sister is dead, then?" you ask.

"She died just two years ago, and it is of her death that I wish to speak to you. Living as we did, we rarely saw friends or loved ones. We had, however, an aunt, Miss Honoria Westphail. We sometimes visited her house. Julia went there at Christmas two years ago. She met a major of marines and became engaged. My stepfather learned of the engagement when my sister returned. He offered no objection to the marriage. But then the terrible event occurred: my sister's tragic death."

You lean back in your chair. "Please, share all of the details," you say.

Miss Stoner goes on. "Every event of that dreadful time is stuck within my memory. The house is very old. The bedrooms are beside each other on the ground floor. The first is Dr. Roylott's, the second my sister's, and the third my own. There are no doors between them, but they all open into the same corridor. Do I make myself plain to you?"

"Perfectly so."

"The windows of the three rooms open out upon the lawn. On that fatal night, Dr. Roylott had gone to his room early, though we knew he had not gone to sleep. My sister could smell his cigar. She left her room and came into mine, where she sat for some time, chatting about her wedding plans. At eleven o'clock she rose to leave, but she paused at the door and looked back.

"'Tell me, Helen,' she said. 'Have you ever heard anyone whistle in the dead of the night?'

"'Never,' said I.

"'I suppose that you don't whistle in your sleep?'

"'Certainly not. Why?'

"'Because during the last few nights I have heard a low whistle. I am a light sleeper, and it has awakened me. I cannot tell where it came from. Perhaps from the next room, perhaps from the lawn. I thought that I would just ask you whether you had heard it.'

"'No, I have not,' said I.

"'I wonder why you did not hear it also.'

"'I sleep more heavily than you.'

"'Well, it is not important.' She smiled back at me, closed my door, and a few moments later I heard her key turn in the lock."

"Indeed," you say. "Was it your custom to lock yourselves in at night?"

"Always."

"And why?"

"I think I mentioned that the doctor kept a cheetah and a baboon. We had no feeling of security unless our doors were locked."

"Quite so. Proceed with your statement."

"I'm sorry," she says. "Before I do, may I try you with one more test? This is a matter of life and death."

You nod and say, "One more test? I do not mind at all, Miss Stoner."

"Thank you, although I am uncertain what to ask. I wonder, I suppose, if you can tell me any more about my journey here."

"There is no mystery, my dear madam," you say, smiling. "The left arm of your jacket is spattered with mud in no less than seven places."

She eagerly looks on, awaiting further explanation.

If you believe the mud means that Miss Stoner rode on a dog-cart, turn to page 110.

If you believe the mud means that Miss Stoner walked from the train station, turn to page 92.

Everything Miss Stoner has described points to the gypsies. They seem to be the only people with whom Dr. Roylott is friendly, and Julia Stoner's dying words about a "speckled band" could very well describe the gypsies' scarves.

You direct Miss Stoner back to the manor, and you promise to return with news of what you find.

"Now, Watson," you say, "we pay the gypsies a visit."

**Go to the next page.**

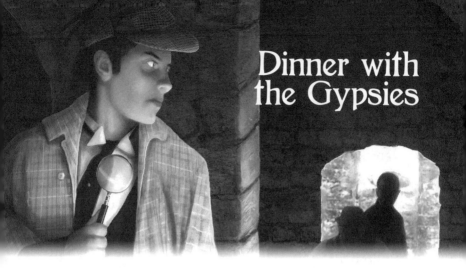

# Dinner with the Gypsies

It takes longer than you anticipate to find the gypsy camp along the border of Stoke Moran's property. You and Watson emerge from the trees into a clearing. Two young girls hide shyly behind the brightly colored skirt of a woman, who tends a pot hanging above a cook fire.

She looks at you and smiles. "Come." She waves you and Watson closer. "We have been expecting you."

Wagons line the edges of the clearing. Other gypsies emerge from behind them. Soon the clearing is filled with the bright clothing and chatter of the gypsy clan.

"I wish to talk with you about the death of Julia Stoner," you announce.

A hush falls over the group.

"First, you eat," replies the woman at the fire. She dishes two steaming bowls of soup. The little girls give one to you and one to Watson.

"Never pass up a good meal," Watson cheerfully declares. He digs into his soup.

You sigh deeply. The sun is close to setting, and you still have no answers. You have not even been able to ask the questions. Out of the corner of your eye, you notice a young gypsy boy run into the forest in the direction of Stoke Moran.

You quickly consume your meal as the gypsies settle around you in a rough circle.

"May we now speak of Julia Stoner?" you ask.

The woman, who seems to speak for the entire group, says, "Perhaps."

You ask your questions but receive no better answers than "maybe" and "perhaps."

Eventually, you have no choice but to give up. You and Watson thank the gypsies for their hospitality and take your leave.

It is too late to go back to Stoke Moran; Dr. Roylott will have returned by now. Frustrated, you and Watson check into the nearby Crown Inn for the night. You are on the upper floor. From your window, you can view Stoke Moran Manor House. You and your partner take turns watching for any mischief.

The night passes, however, without incident.

**Go to the next page.**

At breakfast the next morning, the innkeeper leans over your table and whispers, "Did you hear?"

"Hear what?" asks Watson.

The innkeeper looks around as if to make sure no one else is listening. "That Miss Stoner—the one that lives up at Stoke Moran—she met the same fate as her sister, she did. And just last night too. Creepy business if you ask me."

You leap out of your chair. "Are you positive?"

"Of course," says the innkeeper, suddenly guarded. "But you didn't hear it from me." He bustles to another table, no doubt to spread the sad news of Miss Stoner's untimely death.

Watson says the words, the ones that will haunt you until the end of your days. "Holmes, we're too late."

**Turn to page 68.**

"Your case, Colonel Rairy, is most intriguing," you say. "But I must withdraw from it. You shall have my utmost secrecy, of course."

Surprise flickers across his face. "May I ask why?"

You lean back in your chair. "There are two reasons, actually. The first is that I typically do not delve into cases involving national security. I find civil cases much more suited to my talents. The second is the specific time frame you have requested. I work better when left to my own schedule. Now, I have no doubt you shall soon find the right investigator, and I wish you only the best of luck, sir."

You shake Colonel Rairy's hand, escort him to the door and bid him farewell.

Upon the colonel's departure, Dr. Watson remarks, "Rairy did present an interesting case, didn't he? But I believe you made the right choice, Holmes."

You smile. "As do I, my friend, and I sense we shall have many more interesting cases to come."

**Turn to page 51.**

"I believe the answers to our questions lie with that man," you whisper.

As quietly as possible, you and Watson hurry across the lawn in pursuit of the shadowy figure. He enters the thick woods, and you follow cautiously. The darkness of the forest closes around you. You travel deeper into the woods. Thorns tear at your cloak, and roots reach up to trip you. The figure always stays just ahead.

At last your quarry stops, looking this way and that. Carefully, you draw closer. A shaft of moonlight pierces through the moving leaves and you gasp. The figure you have been chasing is not a man at all. Dr. Roylott's baboon stares back at you. It screeches in terror and takes off into the trees.

A twig snaps behind you. You and Watson turn slowly. Too late, you remember that the baboon is not the only animal to roam the grounds. The last sights you see are the fearsome fangs of a hungry cheetah. There is a sharp pain. A terror-filled cry. Then everything fades to nothingness.

**Turn to page 68.**

"Of course, Miss Stoner," you decide. "Anything you show me could be of the utmost importance."

She leads you and Watson into the hallway and to the room she used to occupy. You spend the better part of an hour studying all that Miss Stoner has to share with you.

She leads you to another room and another. Time escapes you. You are puzzled by this mystery, obsessed with the need to solve it.

Suddenly, thundering footsteps rock the floor. You turn in time to see Dr. Roylott charging at you. He grabs you with one of his large hands, Watson in the other.

"You are not welcome here!" he bellows.

He drags you both to the door and throws you down the front steps with a cry of pure rage. The door slams hard enough to cause a crack in the frame.

You only hope that Miss Stoner has locked herself in her room to escape Dr. Roylott's vicious temper.

**Go to the next page.**

Over the course of the next several weeks, you try in vain to contact your client. Each attempt is expertly blocked by Dr. Roylott.

One morning, you sit in your home office reading the daily newspaper, as is your custom. There, in the death notices, is a familiar name: Helen Stoner.

Your stomach drops. Although you can only guess at the cause of her death, you do know one thing. If you had made better choices, Miss Stoner may still be alive today. It is a knowledge that will haunt you for the rest of your life.

**Turn to page 68.**

There is a long silence. You lean your chin upon your hands and stare into the crackling fire. Watson has never steered you wrong before.

"Your tale is quite interesting, Miss Stoner," you say. "But I fear that's all it is—a tale."

You stand, cross to the door, and pull it open. Miss Stoner looks from you to Watson and back again. She rises hesitantly from her chair.

"I– I don't understand," she says.

"Give Professor Moriarty my regards," you tell her.

"Professor who?" asks Miss Stoner, tears welling in her eyes.

"Ah, you play the part well, madam." You grab her by the shoulder and guide her out the door, closing it behind her.

"I think you made a wise decision, Holmes," says Dr. Watson. "Baboons? Gypsies? Spotted bands? Who knows where Moriarty would have led you."

You nod in agreement.

**Go to the next page.**

You sit in your office, reading the morning newspaper. A week has gone by; you have all but forgotten Miss Helen Stoner.

Until you read her name in the death notices.

Your stomach drops. Helen Stoner is dead, and the circumstances surrounding her death are eerily similar to those of Julia, her sister. Miss Stoner had been telling you the truth.

You could have helped her. Instead, you let your fear of Moriarty get in the way of reason. Her name burns into your brain. Guilt gnaws at your heart.

With shaking hands you remove the sign "Sherlock Holmes, Consulting Detective" from your door. As of this moment, you are retired. You will never take a case again.

**Turn to page 68.**

# Danger in
# the Dark

At dusk you see Dr. Grimesby Roylott drive past. A few minutes later, you see a light spring up among the trees as the lamp is lit in one of the sitting rooms.

"Do you know, Watson," you say. "I question taking you tonight. There is a distinct element of danger."

"Can I be of assistance?"

"Your presence might be invaluable."

"Then I shall certainly come."

"It is very kind of you."

"You speak of danger," says Watson. "You have seen more in these rooms than was visible to me."

"No, but I may have deduced a little more. I imagine you saw all that I did."

"I saw nothing remarkable but the bell-rope. I can not imagine its purpose."

"You saw the ventilator, too?"

"Yes, but I do not think that it is unusual to have a small opening between two rooms. It was so small that a rat could hardly pass through. What harm can there be in that?"

"Well, there is at least a curious coincidence of dates. A ventilator is made, a cord is hung, and a lady who sleeps in the bed dies. Doesn't that strike you?"

"I cannot as yet see any connection."

"Did you observe anything peculiar about that bed?"

"No."

"It was clamped to the floor. The lady could not move her bed. It must always be near the ventilator and the rope." You pause for a moment, then add, "When a doctor goes wrong he is the best of criminals. He has nerve, and he has knowledge. We shall see horrors before the night is over."

**Go to the next page.**

At about nine o'clock, the last light among the trees is extinguished, and all is dark in the direction of the Manor House.

Two hours pass slowly away. Then suddenly, just at the stroke of eleven, a single bright light shines out right in front of you.

"That is our signal," you say, springing to your feet.

A moment later, you are out on the dark road, a chill wind blowing in your face. There is no difficulty in entering the grounds, for you find a large hole in the gate. You make your way among the trees. You reach the lawn and cross it. You are about to enter through the window.

Suddenly, a hideous and distorted person darts out from a clump of bushes. He throws himself upon the grass and then runs swiftly across the lawn into the darkness. "Did you see it?" whispers Watson.

You are startled. Your hand closes upon Watson's left wrist.

Could this be the criminal you seek? Is this the monster behind Dr. Roylott's evil plan? Or does it have nothing to do with his scheme? Should you follow the shadowy figure? Or should you continue inside? The right choice may lead to a solution; the wrong choice could end in disaster. What will you choose to do?

To follow that person, turn to page 130.

To sneak inside the mansion, turn to page 86.

You grab your club from the pocket of your coat and wave it at Colonel Rairy. "The only thing we shall be examining is how your plan failed."

Watson rushes to your side. "What are you doing, Holmes?" he exclaims.

"Do you care to explain, or shall I?" you ask Rairy.

A wide grin spreads slowly across his face. With one swift move, he turns and follows his female companion through the door.

A moment later, he reappears, holding a revolver. You suddenly find yourself looking straight down the barrel of a gun.

"Drop your weapon," says Rairy.

Reluctantly, you let the club clatter to the floor.

"I don't understand," says Watson. "What's all this about, Holmes?"

You keep your voice steady and calm. "Our client is actually the famed Professor Moriarty."

"Well done, Holmes," says the villain. "You reasoned it out. I wish I could be as quick and clever as you." He steps back in mock surprise, holding a hand to his chest. "Oh, wait, I am!"

Moriarty nods his head toward the door, keeping the revolver pointed straight at you. "Move it."

You and Watson are forced outside and into the night's darkness. Your life is at an end, and you know it. You can imagine the coming newspaper headline: FAMED DETECTIVE MISSING, WORST FEARED.

Indeed, it is the worst. You are Sherlock Holmes, Consulting Detective, and because you chose poorly, you will never be heard from again.

**Turn to page 68.**

You lash out at the rope with your knife. "You see it, Watson?" you yell. "You see it?"

"What, Holmes? What?" replies Watson.

You could end this case in an instant, yet your knife cannot find its target. Your plan is not going well.

You suddenly feel a sharp pain. Before the world fades to black, you realize with dread that the Case of the Speckled Band will be your last.

**Turn to page 68.**

"I have seen enough now, Miss Stoner," you decide. "With your permission we shall walk out on the lawn."

Your face is grim as you turn from the scene of this investigation. You walk several times up and down the lawn. Finally you say, "It is very important, Miss Stoner, that you should follow my advice in every respect."

"I shall most certainly do so."

"The matter is too serious for any hesitation. Your life may depend upon it."

"I assure you that I am in your hands."

"In the first place, both my friend and I must spend the night in your room. Let me explain. I believe the village inn is over there?"

"Yes, that is the Crown Inn."

"Your windows would be visible from there?"

"Certainly."

"You must confine yourself to your room when your stepfather comes back. When you hear him retire for the night, you must open the shutters of your window. Put your lamp there as a signal to us, and then sneak quietly into the room you used to occupy. I have no doubt that you could manage there for one night."

"Oh, yes, easily."

"The rest you will leave in our hands. We shall spend the night in your room, and we shall investigate the cause of this noise which has disturbed you."

"I believe that you have already made up your mind," says Miss Stoner.

"Perhaps I have."

"Then, for pity's sake, tell me what was the cause of my sister's death."

"I should prefer to have clearer proof first."

"You can at least tell me whether my own thought is correct. Did she die from some sudden fright?"

"No, I do not think so. There was probably a more tangible cause. And now, Miss Stoner, we must leave you. If Dr. Roylott returned and saw us, our journey would be for nothing. Goodbye, and be brave. We shall soon drive away the dangers that threaten you."

**Go to the next page.**

You have no difficulty in getting a room at the Crown Inn. You are on the upper floor. From your window, you can view Stoke Moran Manor House. While you wait, you must decide upon a weapon for tonight's adventure.

**Turn to page 102.**

You lash furiously with your club at the rope. "You see it, Watson?" you yell. "You see it?"

At that moment, you hear a low, clear whistle. You stop your attack and gaze up at the ventilator.

A moment later, the silence is broken by a most horrible cry. You stand gazing at Watson, and he at you. Finally, the last echoes of it die away into the silence.

"What can it mean?" gasps Watson.

"It means that it is over," you answer. "We will enter Dr. Roylott's room."

You light your lamp and lead the way down the corridor. Twice you knock at the chamber door without any reply from within. You turn the handle and enter, while Watson follows.

A dark-lantern stands on the table. The shutter is half open, throwing a brilliant beam of light upon the iron safe. Its door is open. Beside this table, on the wooden chair, sits Dr. Grimesby Roylott. He is clad in a long gray robe, his feet thrust into red slippers. Across his lap lies the dog whip with the long lash. His chin is arched upward, and his eyes are fixed in a dreadful stare. Above his brow, he wears a peculiar yellow band, with brown speckles. It seems to be bound tightly around his head.

You enter, making neither sound nor motion. "The band, the speckled band," you whisper.

Dr. Roylott's strange headgear begins to move.

Appearing from within his hair, the squat diamond-shaped head and puffed neck of a loathsome serpent hisses at you.

"It is a swamp adder," you shout, "the deadliest snake in all of India!"

"Dr. Roylott has been bitten," notes Watson.

You nod. "Yes, and the poison has already done its worst. The villain has fallen into his own trap. Let us thrust this creature back into its den. We can then move Miss Stoner to some place of shelter and let the police know what has happened here."

You draw the dog-whip swiftly and throw the noose around the reptile's neck. You lift it from its horrid perch and, carrying it at arm's length, enclose it in the iron safe.

You break the sad news to the terrified girl, and you send her by the morning train to see her good aunt in Harrow. You tell your tale to the police. Then you travel home the next day. There, you share with Watson what little he has yet to learn.

"I had come to an entirely wrong conclusion. It shows, my dear Watson, how dangerous it is to reason without enough data. The presence of the gypsies and the use of the word *band* put me upon an entirely wrong trail. I only reconsidered when it became clear that the danger could not come from the window or from the door.

"My attention was drawn to the ventilator and to the bell-rope, which hung down to the bed. The discovery that the bed was clamped to the floor caused me to suspect that the rope was a bridge for something passing through the hole. The idea of a snake occurred to me. When I coupled it with my knowledge that the doctor kept creatures from India, I felt that I was probably on the right track.

"Then I thought of the whistle. Of course, he must recall the snake before the morning light. He had trained it, by the use of milk, to return to him when called. He would put it through the ventilator with the certainty that it would crawl down the rope and land on the bed.

"I had come to these conclusions before I entered his room. An inspection of his chair showed me that he had been standing on it, which would be necessary to reach the ventilator. The safe, the saucer of milk, and the loop of whipcord were enough to dispel any doubts. The metallic clang heard by Miss Stoner was obviously caused by her stepfather closing the door of his safe. Having made up my mind, you know the steps I took to prove the matter. I heard the creature hiss, and so I instantly lit the light and attacked it."

"With the result of driving it through the ventilator," notes Watson.

"Causing it to turn upon its master on the other side," you add. "Some of the blows of my club came home and stirred up its temper. It flew upon the first person it saw."

**Turn to page 51.**

You draw a revolver from the pocket of your coat and point it at Colonel Rairy. "The only thing we shall be examining is how your plan failed."

"What?" Watson and Rairy exclaim in unison.

"Would you care to explain?" you ask Rairy. "Or should I?"

His reply is a sinister scowl.

"Holmes, what is going on here?" asks Watson.

"All will be explained," you assure your friend.

**Go to the next page.**

You get your prisoner loaded into a carriage, tipping the driver to speed you to a police station. You hold your revolver steady as you bounce along the road. Your captive stares at you with angry eyes.

"You see, Watson, our client here is actually the famed Professor Moriarty. Our esteemed professor was not very inventive when constructing his new name. If you sort the letters in *Tom Rairy* differently, they spell *Moriarty*."

"Surely that wasn't the only clue," says Watson.

"Of course, not," you reply. "But it was enough to arouse suspicion. I also found it rather obvious that Colonel Rairy is no colonel at all. His shaggy beard is perfectly suited for a disguise, but it is not the beard of a military man."

"Indeed!" says your friend.

"Our villain also made a mistake when he saluted me. As you well know, Watson, military men may salute one another, but they would never salute an ordinary citizen, such as myself."

"Well done, Holmes," says Dr. Watson. "I would call this case a success!"

Across from you, Moriarty snorts. "A minor setback, Sherlock Holmes. Sooner or later you will fail, and I will celebrate your downfall."

You smile confidently. "Perhaps some day, Professor, but not tonight."

**Turn to page 51.**

# Epilogue

You snap to alertness, shaking the cobwebs from your mind. You scan your dark surroundings. It takes a moment for your eyes to adjust, but you realize you're back in Uncle Barry's dimly lit attic, *The Adventures of Sherlock Holmes* still clutched in your hands.

Was it all just a dream? It doesn't seem like it. Your mind feels awakened like never before; you are strangely aware of yourself and your environment. You feel oddly excited to get back to your study room. That math homework—those word problems—are no longer chores that have been forced upon you. Instead, you see them as mysteries waiting to be solved.

You step carefully back to the opening in the attic floor. You slide slowly downward until your feet make contact with the bathroom sink. You climb out of the attic, pop the wooden panel back into place, and hop to the floor.

You confidently hurry back to your study room and sit at your desk. You read the problem that has been troubling you, and you smile. The answer doesn't come directly to you, but you now see the clues—and you know how to put them together. You grab your pencil, and you begin to write.

You take comfort in knowing that life is a series of mysteries. You cannot wait to get started, gathering clues and looking for answers. It may not always be easy, but it's sure to be a lot of fun.

**Go to the next page.**

# The End

**You have survived the adventures of Sherlock Holmes!**

# CAN YOU SURVIVE THESE STORIES?

Test your survival skills with a free
short story at www.Lake7Creative.com

and pick up these
Choose Your Path books:

# About Sir Arthur

Arthur Doyle was born in Edinburgh, Scotland, on May 22, 1859. His family was poor, but his mother had a passion for reading and storytelling. Doyle discovered that he had a gift for storytelling too.

When he was 17, Doyle began studying medicine. He also started publishing short stories in magazines. His first book, *A Study in Scarlet*, was published in 1888 and introduced the world to the characters of Sherlock Holmes and Dr. Watson. The book was an instant hit. In 1891, Doyle gave up his medical practice to become a full-time author.

In 1902, Doyle wrote about Great Britain's war in South Africa, and his words helped gain support for his country. This was so important that King Edward VII made Doyle a knight. From then on, the author became known as "Sir" Arthur Conan Doyle.

Doyle died on July 7, 1930, leaving behind perhaps the most famous character in history. His adventures still capture our imaginations today.

# About His Book

Before *The Adventures of Sherlock Holmes* became a book, it was published as a series of twelve short stories. *The Strand Magazine* in the United Kingdom ran the tales from July 1891 to June 1892. They were so popular that the magazine's founder, George Newnes, decided to publish them as a book in October 1892.

Many people believe Sherlock Holmes resembled Dr. Joseph Bell, a teacher at Edinburgh University. The doctor was described as intensely observant, often correctly diagnosing patients before they even said a word. Doyle was only 17 years old when he met Dr. Bell. But when *The Adventures of Sherlock Holmes* was published 16 years later, Doyle dedicated the book to the doctor who made such an impression on him.

This version of *The Adventures of Sherlock Holmes* adapts three of the twelve original stories, and it is with the greatest of respect for Sir Arthur Conan Doyle that we present them here as choose your path adventures.

# About Ryan Jacobson

Ryan Jacobson has always loved choose your path books, so he is thrilled to get a chance to write them. He used his memories of those fun-filled stories and his past experiences to write *Lost in the Wild*. The book became so popular that he followed it with *Storm at the Summit of Mount Everest* and the *Can You Survive?* series of adaptations.

Ryan is the author of more than 20 books, including picture books, comics, graphic novels, chapter books and ghost stories. He lives in Mora, Minnesota, with his wife Lora, sons Jonah and Lucas, and dog Boo.

For more details, visit RyanJacobsonOnline.com.

# About Deb Mercier

Being a mother, Deb Mercier's main job seems to be picking things up, but she also loves the outdoors and solving life's daily mysteries. She writes children's books, as well as humor essays for adults. Her writing credits include several middle-grade books (including choose your path books), two picture books and a long-running newspaper column.

Deb and her family live in rural Minnesota. She volunteers at Minnewaska Area Schools, loves pizza and saves turtles from roadways whenever possible. For more information about Deb and her latest projects, please visit www.debmercier.com.